3

CONTENTS

No time to waste

With their hearts pounding like drums, Evan and Conor rushed to Grandad's front door for another adventure in Dragonterra. Ever since he had told them about the secret portal in his garden, they longed for their next visit to Grandad's house!

They had already travelled to the magical land of Dragonterra twice. The first time, they discovered a real dragon, hidden in an underground cave. During their second mission, they found one of her eggs on a remote island. But there were still four more eggs to find. They desperately hoped that today they would search for another one.

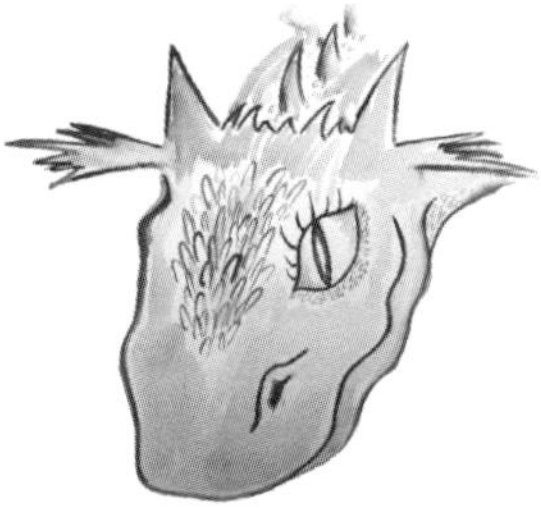

Dad had no idea about their

adventures in Dragonterra. It was a secret that they shared only with Grandad. Smiling happily, Dad waved at them from the car. "Have a good day, boys," he called. "Don't be pestering Grandad too much! Stay off that iPad and entertain yourselves outside in the fresh Donegal air!"

The boys grinned at each other. "We'll be sure to stay out of Grandad's way," they replied merrily.

Grandad greeted the boys with a hug and led them inside without delay. As they entered the sitting room, they could see that he had the brown rucksack packed and ready for their adventure in Dragonterra. It contained all sorts of magical objects that the boys might need to help them during their quest.

On the table, the little oval-shaped stone was glowing brightly; a sign that Lucy the wozlett was waiting for them to return to Dragonterra as soon as possible.

"I'm so glad you're finally here, boys," said Grandad. "Lucy will be growing more impatient by the minute!"

The boys smiled. Lucy the wozlett was a little creature with a big personality. She guided them through Dragonterra and helped them on their missions. Although she could get rather cranky, she was a good friend to the boys by now.

"I'm ready to go, Grandad!" said Evan bravely. It was an exciting place, but the nasty ruler of Dragonterra, Wizard Snivvard, tried his best to make it a scary place for the boys, too. He didn't want them to find the dragon eggs. In fact, it

was Snivvard who had stolen the eggs from a dragon named Aleeze. The boys needed to find all five of her eggs to break Snivvard's spell so that the mighty dragons could rule over Dragonterra once more.

"You are both doing such a fantastic job," said Grandad proudly. "I feel like a boy again, just hearing about your adventures in Dragonterra." Grandad had been to Dragonterra as a boy and had managed to rescue one dragon egg. That egg had hatched and grown up to become the last dragon in Dragonterra - Aleeze. Now, many years later, he longed for Evan and Conor to find all five of her eggs... and he was sure they could do it!

"I'm ready too!" cried Conor. "I can't wait to see where exactly the portal will lead to this time!"

"And what creatures we will meet along the way!" added Evan excitedly.

"Don't forget to keep an eye out for Wizard Snivvard," warned Grandad. "Remember, he can't harm you. His nasty magic won't work on you because you come from another world, but he will try his best to scare you instead."

"Don't worry, Grandad," replied

Conor confidently. "We are getting used to his tricks!"

With that, they hurried through the long grass in Grandad's back garden towards the old stone wall. As always, Grandad had the glowing beacon ready. He tapped it against the smooth, grey rock to reveal the secret portal to Dragonterra. "Have fun, boys," called Grandad as they stepped forward, "but be careful, too!"

Whoosh!!! Evan and Conor tumbled through the air as the humming sound of the portal filled their ears. In the dazzling glare of the portal, the boys could see swirling shades of purple this time. It seemed like they were doing cartwheels in a field of lavender. And then suddenly, their feet touched down in the land of Dragonterra once more.

Up, up and away!

This time, the ground beneath them felt very firm. Conor stamped his foot to test it out. "Ouch!" he yelped, as the impact hurt his ankle.

"What did you think would happen?" snapped a cranky little voice. "That's solid rock, you know."

Both boys' faces lit up. "Lucy!" they cried, delighted to see their furry little companion again. "Where are we this time?" asked Evan, looking around in amazement. Lucy scampered up his leg and perched on his shoulder. "We're in the Rugged Mountains of Dragonterra today," she explained. All around them, enormous mountains stretched up into the clouds.

"We've already searched the forest

and the islands," said Lucy, "so it's time to search the mountains for another of the eggs. All we can do is wander around and hope for the best," she added with a sigh. The boys' faces grew pale. Stretching out in every direction were mountains that seemed ten times bigger than Mount Errigal - and that was the tallest mountain in Donegal!

Lucy began to laugh. "Okay, okay," she giggled, "we don't have to search the mountains on foot! I brought something special along with me." With that, she pointed proudly at a large wooden basket with a white sheet of fabric folded neatly beside it. The boys had no idea what it was or how it would help them to explore the mountains.

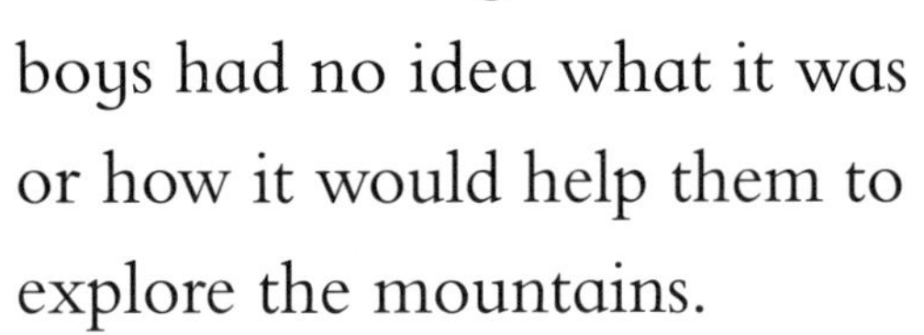

"What is it?" asked Conor, causing Lucy to roll her eyes.

"It's a magic air balloon, of course! It's a bit like a hot air balloon, but the air that makes it rise isn't hot – it's magic!" Her eyes twinkled with delight.

"Where will we get the magic air to

make it fly?" asked Evan, still as confused as ever.

"In the rucksack your grandad gave you," she sighed. The boys weren't sure how there could be magic air in the rucksack, but they knew that Lucy would get cranky if they asked too many questions.

"Open the rucksack and look for a little straw. It will help us to get this magic air balloon in the sky!" she exclaimed. Conor rummaged around in the bag and pulled out a thin, black straw.

"Excellent!" cried Lucy. "Now, crawl under the white sheet of fabric, take a deep breath, and blow as hard as you can through the straw."

Conor did as he was told. As he blew, the straw glowed brightly in his hands. The magic was working! Sure enough, the fabric began to rise up into the air and puffed out into the shape of a giant balloon. Lucy clapped her little paws together in delight. "Now, hop into the basket before it lifts off the ground!" she cheered. "Up, up and away!"

Here comes trouble!

The magic air balloon rose quickly into the sky and the huge rocks far below them now resembled tiny pebbles. Soon, they were up so high that wispy clouds floated past them.

As the magic air balloon soared over the mountains, they all peered down, looking for anything unusual that might suggest an egg had been hidden in the area. It was a difficult task, but they knew they had to try their best to find an egg. The future of the dragons depended on it!

"This is tricky," sighed Conor after a while. "Yes," agreed Lucy. "The egg looks quite like a rock, so it will blend in here in the mountains; that will

make it very difficult to find."

The boys had already seen one of Aleeze's eggs. It was larger than a football and as black as the night sky, like a lump of coal.

Suddenly, a buzzing sound interrupted their conversation. "What's that?" asked Evan in alarm, pointing at a large insect hovering right beside him. It was blue with lime green spots all over. It had a flat, piggy nose and a very pointy rear end.

"Yikes!" squealed Lucy. "That's a sambleboo! They can sting!" She scrambled onto Evan's shoulder and dived into his hood for cover. "I don't understand why it is buzzing around up here in the

clouds," she added, peeking her head out cautiously.

The buzzing sound grew louder and before they knew it, dozens of sambleboos swarmed around the magic air balloon. "Something strange is going on," whispered Lucy.

"Snivvard!" cried Conor, as he spotted the wizard floating on a little cloud of mist nearby. He had his arms folded, his wispy beard was blowing in the breeze, and he had a nasty grin on his face.

"He must have cast a spell on the sambleboos!" gasped Lucy. The boys felt a surge of panic. "Will those insects sting us?" shouted Evan in alarm. "I was stung by a bee once and it

was very sore! I really don't want to get stung by a sambleboo!"

"Don't worry," replied Lucy. "Snivvard can't use his magic to hurt you, but they could sting me!" she added, ducking down into Evan's hood again.

"I wonder what his plan is?" asked Conor, trembling a little. Snivvard clapped his hands together. It sounded like thunder. All of the sambleboos

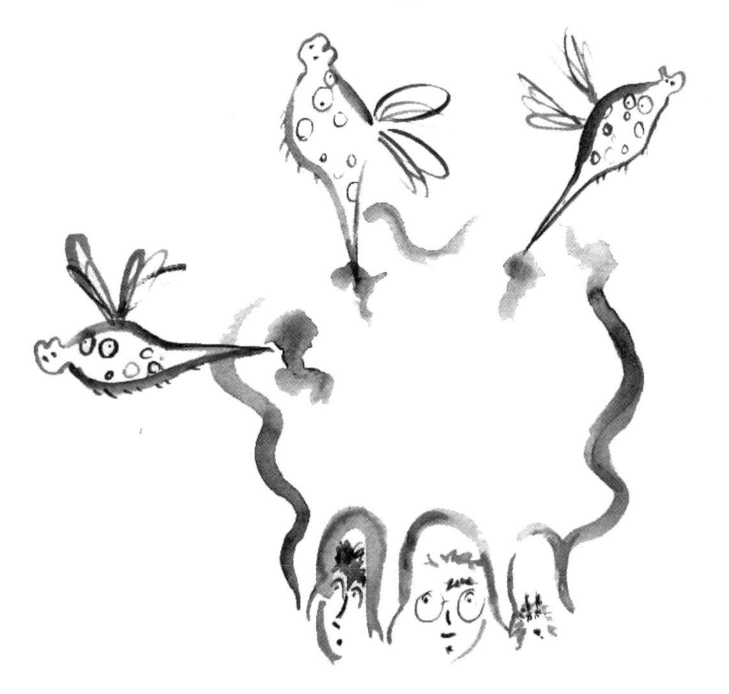

suddenly began flying angrily at the white fabric, tearing holes in it with their pointy rear ends! The magic air balloon began to sink down towards the ground.

"So that's his plan," moaned Lucy. "He is destroying our magic air balloon!"

Snivvard cackled loudly and rubbed his bony grey hands together with glee.

Down, down, down drifted the magic air balloon. Soon, they were far below Snivvard and the sound of his nasty laugh grew faint. The wooden basket landed on the ground with a thud and everyone jumped out safely.

"We have no choice but to explore the area on foot now," sighed Lucy. "The good news is, we must be very near an egg if Snivvard is trying to stop us!"

'Knot' a problem!

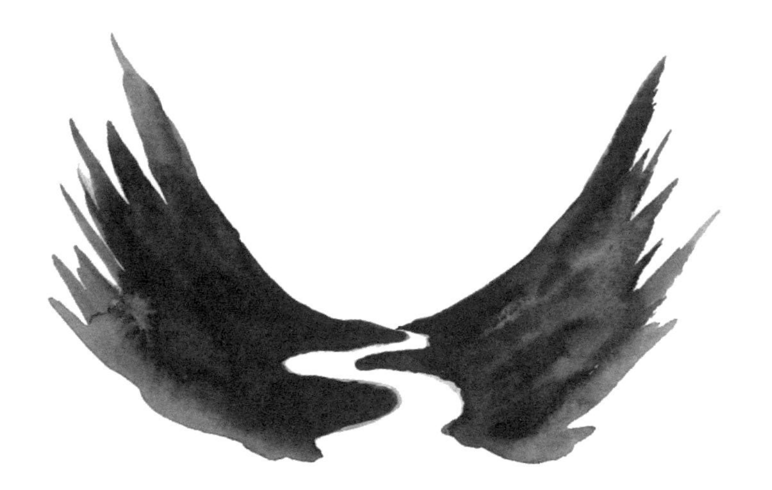

The boys spotted a little path leading through the mountains. "Once, we climbed Muckish Mountain with Mum and Dad, and Grandad advised us to stick to the path," said Evan.

"Yes," chirped Lucy, "that's sound advice. Let's go - there's no time to waste!"

Setting off along the mountain path, they searched all around for any signs of an egg, but they could see nothing apart from grey rocks and a few scrawny trees.

Suddenly, another strange noise echoed all around them.

"Blaaaaaaalll!"

"That sounds a bit like a sheep," exclaimed Conor in surprise.

"Could it be another of Snivvard's tricks?" asked Evan with a frown.

"I'm not sure," replied Lucy. "Let's go have a look, but we'll stay out of sight!" Peeking out from behind a big rock, they spotted a dozen creatures running around in circles. They were quite like sheep, but their woolly coats were bright green.

"They look like little bushes with legs!" whispered Conor. Evan gave a chuckle and nodded in agreement.

"Oh, they're waydees!" smiled Lucy.

"They're completely harmless, but they seem to be in a bit of a panic," she remarked. "We'd better find out what's going on." They hopped over the rock and approached the herd of waydees.

"Is there a problem?" asked Lucy politely. The biggest waydee stepped forward. "A biiiiiiiig problem!" he bleated. "One of our baby waydees has fallen down a deep hole and we can't get her out!" he cried in despair. Lucy peered into the hole and saw a tiny waydee standing at the bottom, all alone and looking very sad indeed.

"Thankfully, she's not injured," continued the biggest waydee, "but we just can't figure out a way to rescue her!"

"Don't worry, we can help," soothed Lucy.

Conor and Evan knew that Lucy would come up with a clever plan. "There should be a magic rope in the rucksack," she explained. Evan rummaged around, but all he could find was a very short piece of twine. "I don't think this will be much help," sighed Evan, holding it up to show Lucy.

"That's exactly what we need!" she cheered. "It might look short now, but remember, it's a magic rope," she added, her eyes sparkling with delight. "All you have to do is hold on to each end and stretch the rope to whatever length you need!"

The waydees began to leap happily in the air. The boys did as they were told, and sure enough, the short rope began to glow brightly with magic. It stretched as easily as homemade slime with the boys pulling firmly on each

end. When it was even longer than their school bus, they stopped pulling the rope. It lost its glow, but it was now the perfect length to rescue the baby waydee.

"Do either of you boys know how to tie a good knot?" asked Lucy hopefully. "I'm not strong enough to tie one with these little paws, but if you do it, I can then climb down and loop it around the baby waydee."

The boys smiled. "Last summer, Grandad brought us to Killybegs and a friendly fisherman taught us how to tie a perfect knot!" grinned Evan.

Lucy's face lit up with happiness. "Grandad has prepared you so well for these missions!" she beamed. Within minutes, the rope was ready. Tugging firmly on the knot, Lucy nodded in approval. "I'll climb down and as soon as I whistle, you boys must work together to pull the baby waydee up and out of the hole! Ready?" she grinned.

"Yes!" chorused the boys.

With that, Lucy scrambled over the edge of the hole with her teeth clenched on the rope. The boys waited nervously to hear her whistle – the signal that they should pull the baby waydee up and out of the hole.

As the minutes ticked by, the herd of waydees started to shuffle around, whispering fretfully. Evan peered carefully over the edge of the hole. "Is everything ok down there?" he called. There wasn't a peep to be heard from Lucy. Conor peeked anxiously into the hole and called out, too. "Lucy, are you ok?" But silence filled the air.

Then, just as the panic was really setting in, Lucy's little voice squeaked up and out of the hole. "You won't BELIEVE what's down here, boys," she yelled excitedly, "... a dragon egg!"

Avalanche!

Suddenly, the sky grew dark as mist began to swirl all around them, blocking out the sun. "Snivvard is back again!" gasped Evan. Sure enough, there he was, floating on his little cloud of mist and looking as angry as ever. "I shall not allow you to get that egg!" he bellowed. He raised his hands in the air and the ground below them started to rumble. Loose pebbles and small stones began to slide into the hole.

"Oh no!" gasped Conor. "Snivvard is starting an avalanche!"

Without delay, they pulled on the rope with all their might to lift the poor baby waydee to safety. Although she looked tiny way down at the bottom of the hole, she was in fact very heavy! The herd of waydees tried to help by gripping the rope with their teeth, but they couldn't hold on for long. It was up to Conor and Evan to save her. With burning hands and aching arms, they continued to pull the rope.

Soon, the baby waydee popped her fluffy, green head up over the edge of the hole. And with one last tug of the rope, she scrambled towards the safety and comfort of her mother.

Lucy followed close behind, her eyes wide with fright and her bushy tail high in the air. The boys breathed a sigh of relief to see Lucy, but they weren't out of danger yet! By now, larger rocks were rolling towards the hole and crashing down on top of the dragon egg.

Lucy gasped. "The egg is as strong as a rock; it won't get damaged, but Snivvard is burying it so that we won't be able to reach it!" More and more giant rocks tumbled down into the hole as Snivvard watched with a nasty grin on his face. Before long, the hole was completely filled in and now looked like a mound of rubble.

Snivvard gave a

long cackle. "You'll never reach the egg now!" he sneered. "Just give up and go home, you little brats!" With that, he vanished in a puff of smoke.

The rumbling stopped as soon as he disappeared. The waydees had been standing back to avoid the crashing rocks, but now they gathered around the boys. "Thank you so much for helping us," gushed the biggest waydee. "We're

not sure what made her go near that dangerous hole in the first place!"

Lucy perched on Conor's shoulder to address the herd of waydees. "I think I know what happened," she began. "As soon as I climbed down into the hole, I could smell coconuts! Baby waydees have a great sense of smell. She must have followed her nose in search of food and tumbled into the hole! But of course, there aren't actually any coconuts growing up here in the mountains - the unusual smell was in fact coming from the dragon egg!"

"Oh, yes!" added Conor. "You already told us that each dragon egg has a different smell!"

Evan nodded. "I'm glad we've located the egg, but now Snivvard has made it impossible to reach," he sighed.

Lucy's eyes sparkled. "Nothing is impossible," she replied. "We'll think of something."

The two boys stood in silence, wondering what plan Lucy could possibly come up with. She paced over and back, scratching her furry little head and muttering to herself. "Aha!" she cheered at last, leaping in the air. "That could work!"

She scrambled up Evan's leg in a flash, unzipped the rucksack, and dived inside for a good rummage around. "Excellent!"

she cried, her little voice muffled inside the bag. Soon, she popped out holding a small black pot with the lid screwed on tightly. "Shrinking dust!" she declared merrily, holding it out to show the boys.

Three tiny adventurers

"Shrinking dust?" repeated Evan, blinking in disbelief. Lucy's eyes twinkled with delight. "Yes, it's exactly that - dust that makes you shrink!"

Conor was still feeling quite confused.

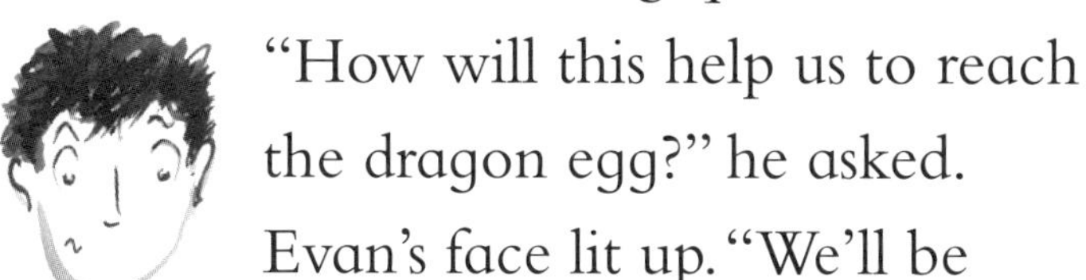

"How will this help us to reach the dragon egg?" he asked.

Evan's face lit up. "We'll be small enough to climb down through the gaps in the rocks!" he gasped.

"Exactly!" Lucy exclaimed.

The boys were excited but also rather nervous.

"Don't worry," soothed Lucy, "I'll lead the way to make sure the path is safe."

"Okay," said Conor bravely, "how does the shrinking dust work?"

Lucy grinned. "We have to stand close

together and sprinkle the dust all around us in a circle. Everything inside the circle of dust will shrink!"

"How will we return to our normal sizes?" asked Evan anxiously.

"The magic will wear off after a while, so we must hurry!" she replied. There was no time to waste. The boys stood back to back, while Lucy perched on their shoulders. Evan carefully unscrewed the lid of the pot and the dust inside began to glow brightly. He sprinkled it all around his feet, before passing it to Conor so that he could do the same on his side.

The waydees watched on, amazed by the glowing dust. "Good luck on your quest!" called the biggest waydee. "And thanks again for your help!"

With that, the boys felt like they were on a rollercoaster. Their bellies did somersaults and their heads were light. "It's working!" cheered Lucy. They closed their eyes as the glow of the magic dust shone brighter. When they opened them, the world looked very different indeed. Blades of grass looked like trees and the waydees now looked like gigantic green monsters – even the little baby!

"Time to scamper into the hole, in case someone squashes us!" squeaked

Lucy. The boys nodded before bravely stepping after her between some rocks. As they moved deeper down through the rubble, the sunlight faded away.

"Lucy?" Evan asked. "Any chance of a bit of light, please?"

Lucy grinned. "Of course! It would be my pleasure." She began shaking her body like a scruffy dog after a swim in the sea. Wiggle, waggle, wiggle, waggle!

The boys watched in amazement as her fur began to glow in the dark. They had seen this before, when they first entered the underground cave, but it was every bit as magical to see it happening again. Lucy was like a little star shining brightly in a dark night sky. It was much easier to follow the golden glow of her fur as they moved deeper into the rubble,

squeezing through narrow gaps along the way.

The smell of coconuts suddenly wafted up Conor's nose. "I can smell the egg!" he whispered excitedly. Evan took a deep breath and had a good sniff, too. "Me too!" he cheered. "We're nearly there!"

They squeezed their way through another few gaps in the rocks. Sure enough, there before them was Aleeze's egg, undamaged by the avalanche. It was enormous, like a pitch-black circus tent looming before them because they were still tiny.

Jumping for joy, everyone was delighted and relieved that the plan had worked. Thanks to the shrinking dust, they had been able to crawl all the way down through the rocks to reach the egg!

"All we have to do now is return it to Aleeze!" cheered Lucy. She took out the little stone that they could use to whoosh back to the dragon. "Remember, close your eyes and think of Aleeze's underground cave and we must all be touching the egg in order to transport it along with us. Ready?"

The boys nodded, touching the stone with one hand and the dragon egg with the other. Whoosh!!! They were transported back to Aleeze's secret hiding place in a flash.

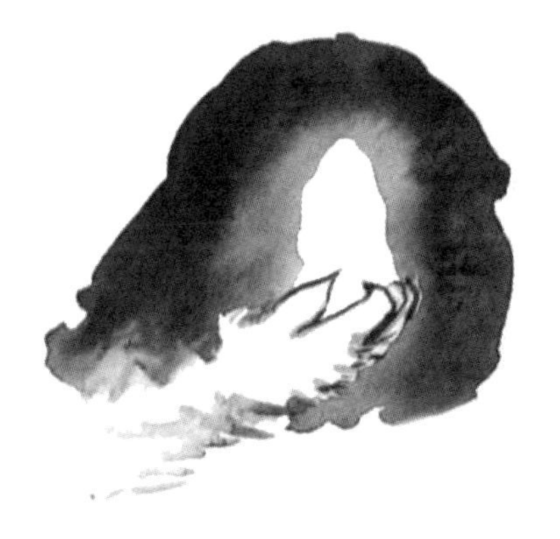

Naming another dragon

Lucy's glowing fur helped them to see in the darkness of Aleeze's cave. The dragon was in a deep sleep again, her mighty nostrils flaring with each steady breath she took.

They gently touched her scaly skin to wake her up and tell her the good news. She could hear their thoughts as long as they were touching her and they could hear hers, too!

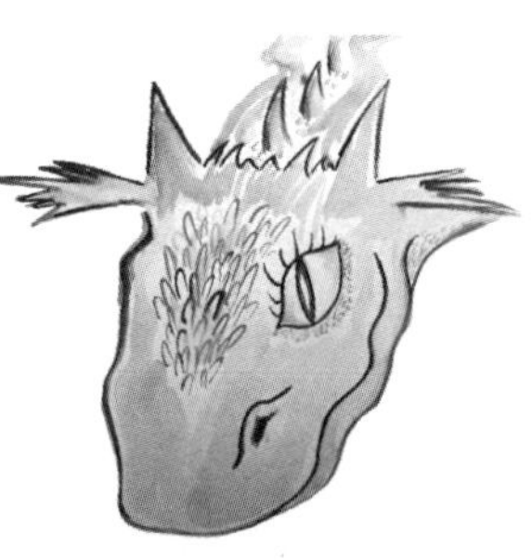

"We're here with another egg!" they repeated over and over in their heads until Aleeze began to stir. Her heavy eyelids blinked open. When she saw the egg, she sprang to her feet with joy. Clouds of dust rose up as she bounced about with excitement.

Aleeze wasn't aware that Lucy, Evan and Conor were all tiny, so they ran for cover in case she accidentally stood on them! They watched in awe as she tenderly nuzzled the egg with her snout and used her tail to push it under her belly to join the other egg already in her care.

Both eggs flickered in shades of red and orange, now that they were back in their nest. Although she was delighted to have two eggs back safely, she looked around anxiously, wondering where Lucy and the boys could be.

Thankfully, at that very moment, the shrinking dust began to wear off. Glowing brightly with magic, they all returned to their normal sizes. Aleeze watched calmly, for magic didn't seem strange or unusual to a dragon! They moved closer and gently touched her snout to speak to her again.

"How can I ever thank you, you wonderful boys?" she

gushed. They both smiled, feeling very proud indeed. "It is a pleasure to help find your eggs, Aleeze," replied Evan.

"We've never had an adventure like this in our whole lives!" added Conor earnestly.

"There are always adventures to be had in Dragonterra," smiled Aleeze. "Now, what name do you think suits this little egg?"

The boys couldn't believe it. They'd

get to pick the name of ANOTHER dragon?! They both thought long and hard for a good name.

"What about Saydee?" suggested Evan at last. "To remind us of today's adventure with the sambleboos and the waydees."

"Perfect!" replied Conor. "As long as you don't mind, Aleeze?"

Aleeze nuzzled the egg again and it glowed even brighter against her warm belly. "Saydee is a beautiful name," she beamed. "So far, we have two eggs - Kipsula and Saydee. I do hope you manage to find the remaining three eggs and pick lovely names for them, too," she added.

"We will try our very best!" said Conor in his most determined voice.

"But for now, you must go home and rest," urged Lucy. "All that rock climbing was exhausting!" The boys nodded in agreement.

"I will do a little more research to find the best location for our next mission," continued Lucy. "The eggs will become even harder to find and Snivvard will come up with more nasty ways to scare us. He'll stop at nothing to prevent us from finding those last three eggs," she sighed.

"How long has Snivvard been the ruler of Dragonterra?" asked Conor. It was Aleeze who answered the question. "Over one hundred years," she whispered sadly. "No one has ever managed to find all five eggs to break the spell. Finding one or two is fantastic, because it gives us a chance to lay more eggs in the future, but the only way to defeat Snivvard, once and for all, is to find all five of them," she added with a tearful sigh.

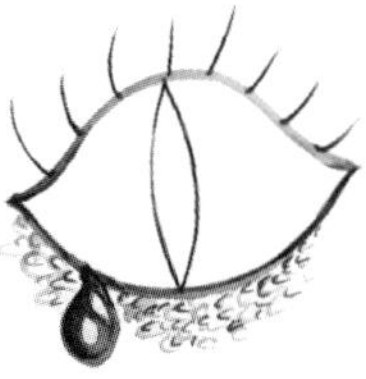

"We've made a great start!" chirped

Lucy cheerfully. "I have a good feeling about these boys from Donegal," she said, nuzzling into both of them. "For now, off you go, and tell Grandad I said hello."

They smiled as they shut their eyes and imagined the portal at the bottom of Grandad's garden. Whoosh!!! The grass made for a soft landing after their rocky adventure in the mountains. They ran towards the house, eager to pass on Lucy's message and also to tell Grandad that the mission had been a success.

He greeted them at the back door and knew straight away from their beaming smiles that they had found another egg. He hugged them both tightly, so proud that they were carrying on the mission that he had started himself, long ago.

"Come in and tell me all about it, boys!" he said cheerfully. "There's even time for a hot chocolate before Dad picks you up!" They snuggled up together, sipping on the yummy hot chocolate and telling Grandad about their wonderful adventures in Dragonterra.

Join Evan, Conor and Lucy on their next mission, to find the third dragon egg, deep in the jungle of Dragonterra. Check out the map on the next page to see its location! What nasty tricks does Snivvard have in store for them? There are many strange and wonderful creatures to meet as they continue to explore the magical land of Dragonterra....

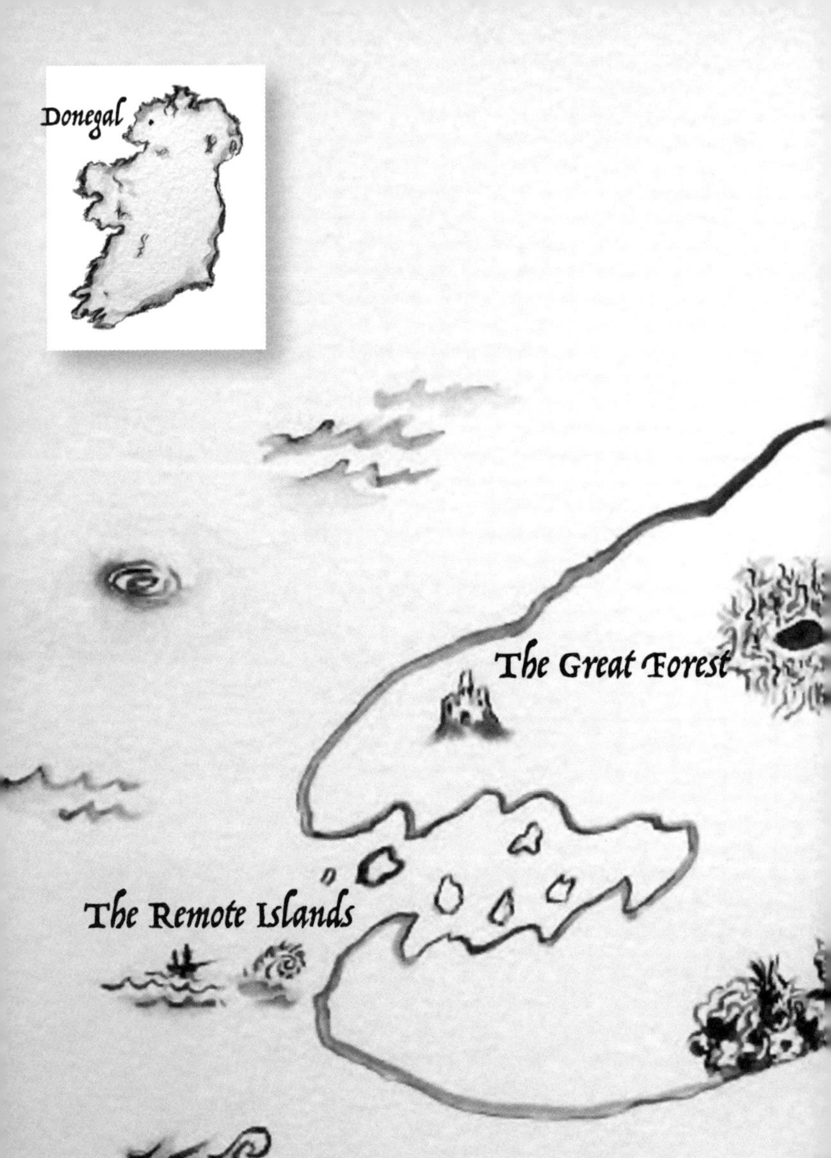
Donegal
The Great Forest
The Remote Islands

The Rugged Mountains
The Far-reaching Jungle